The Doorknob just SMILED at ME

by Linda Coolidge-McKinley
Art by Brittany Trivelli

Published in 2020, by Gypsy Publications
Troy, OH 45373, U.S.A.
www.GypsyPublications.com

Coolidge-McKinley, Linda
The Doorknob Just Smiled at Me
Story by Linda Coolidge-McKinley; Art by Brittany Trivelli

ISBN 978-1-938768-36-1 (paperback)

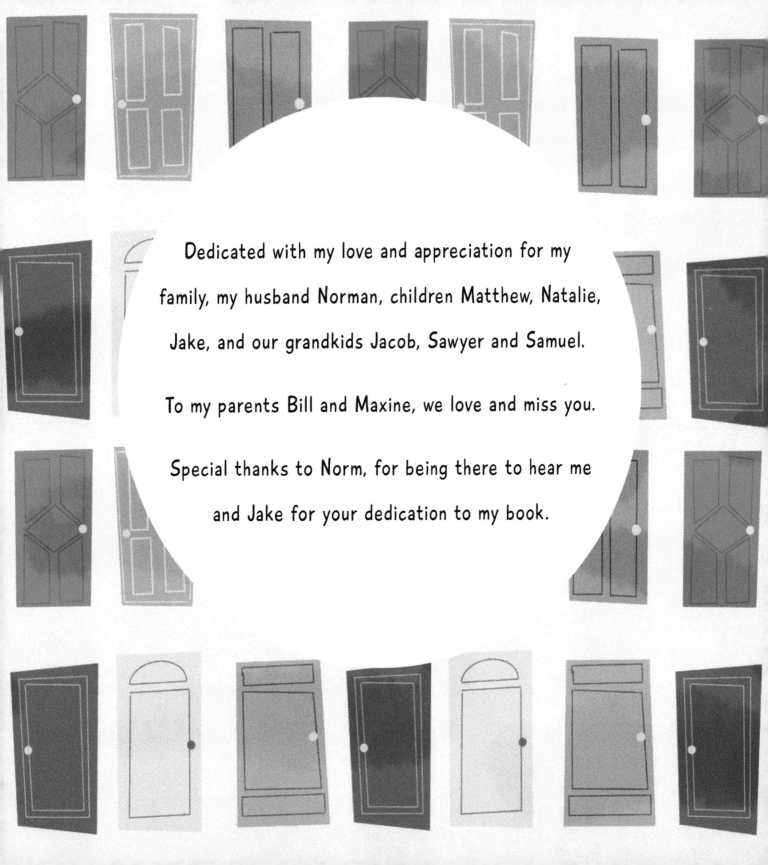

Dedicated with my love and appreciation for my family, my husband Norman, children Matthew, Natalie, Jake, and our grandkids Jacob, Sawyer and Samuel.

To my parents Bill and Maxine, we love and miss you.

Special thanks to Norm, for being there to hear me and Jake for your dedication to my book.

The wind was howling around the corner of the house while Grandma and Grandpa slept. All of a sudden Grandma awoke because of the howling wind.

Walking in her nightgown, she peered out of the window and she saw the trees blowing and the leaves swirling.

Everything looked ok, so she headed back
to bed. As she walked past the front door,
Grandma saw the doorknob smile at her.

She smiled back and went back
to bed, thinking nothing of it.

In the morning over breakfast, Grandma told Grandpa what happened last night. They all jumped up to look at the doorknob, but the doorknob looked grumpy — no smiles today.

As they went on with their day, their grandchildren, Jacob and Suzanne, came over and Grandma and Grandpa told them the amazing news. Excited, the grandchildren ran to the door with the dogs, Luna and Piper.

As usual, Luna got there first and turned the doorknob with her mouth. Much to Jacob's surprise, the door exclaimed "Ouch, you bit me, don't you know I have feelings too!" Luna the dog jumped back and barked, then looked at and sniffed the doorknob with much interest.

Jacob and Suzanne looked at each other with shock as they ran to tell their Grandma and Grandpa what just happened.

Together Grandma and Grandpa
said with dismay, "The doorknob
never talked to us before!"

Grandma explained "You see, I
believe the doorknobs were just
waiting for us to notice them.
We get so busy sometimes we
miss the small things."

So we came inside and started examining all of the doorknobs in the house; we saw that all of the knobs looked and stayed grumpy.

When trick or treat for Halloween came around, Jacob and Suzanne handed out treats to the children dressed up in their scary Halloween outfits.

Much to Jacob and Suzanne's surprise,
the front doorknob came to life yelling,
"Trick or Treat, get out of here you kids,
go boo somewhere else!"
    The kids yelled back, "You are the
grouchiest doorknob in all of town."

The front doorknob was the ring leader of the grouches and the grouchiest of all. He never smiled and made all of the other doorknobs in the house grumpy.

One day Grandpa said, maybe we should take the grouchiest doorknob to the doorknob doctor. So, Grandpa got out his screwdriver and removed the doorknob from the front door.

We all piled into Gramp's car, Grandpa, Grandma, Jacob, and Suzanne.

Grandma held the doorknob safe and sound in the box for the trip to the doorknob doctor.

Once there, Dr. David lifted the grumpy doorknob out of his box and peered closely at the patient.

"Why are you so grumpy? You live in a nice house with nice people, kids, and dogs and yet you remain a grouch, what is wrong?" asked the doctor.

The doorknob responded "No one talks to me, everyone squeezes me too hard, they never give me a bath, and I have this splinter stuck in my knob!"

Dr. David looked with concern at the doorknob, opened his toolkit, removed a set of tweezers, and promptly removed the painful splinter from the doorknob.

Then grandpa responded by saying "We will talk to you, give you a bath, and be careful not to squeeze too hard when we open the door, would that be ok with you?" asked Grandpa. "Yes!" exclaimed grumpy the doorknob.

Grumpy was now so happy and Grandma and Grandpa's house will never be the same. Relatives and neighbors came to gaze at all the happy smiling doorknobs in the house. And at Christmas we opened all of the doors and the joyful doorknobs all sang Christmas songs like a choir to everyone. It was quite a curiosity, but quite a lot of fun!

CPSIA information can be obtained
at www.ICGtesting.com
Printed in the USA
BVHW021757191220
595731BV00004B/80